READY, SET, GO!

Written and Illustrated by Susan Marino

MODERN PUBLISHING
A Division of Unisystems, Inc.
New York, New York 10022

"Ummph!" grunted Hard Boiled as he lifted a heavy barbell over his head.

"Wow! You're really strong, Hard Boiled," Sunny Side Up said to his older brother with admiration.

"It's not so hard, Sunny," Hard Boiled said. "I keep myself in good physical shape."

Sunny Side Up and Hard Boiled were at the local gym.
Their friend, Over Easy, joined them. "Hi, guys, what's up?"
"We just finished working out," Hard Boiled said as he put his
towel in his gym bag and the three friends headed out the door.

As the three walked down the street, Egg Salad, Egg Nog and Egg Cream waved from the opposite side.

"Hi, boys," Egg Salad called. "Guess who we just ran into?"

"Who?" Over Easy asked.

"The Tigers," answered Egg Salad. "They're boasting that they are the greatest club in town."

"But that's not true," said Egg Nog. "We're the best club in town, aren't we, Hard Boiled?"

"Sure we are," Egg Cream interrupted. "Let's show those guys who the best club is!" she exclaimed.

Hard Boiled had been listening closely. "I've got it," he said. "Let's have a challenge day. It'll be like a contest to choose the best club."

"Like the Olympics!" Egg Nog shouted.
"Yeah!" the others joined in. "That's a great idea."

When the Scrambled Eggs presented their plan to the Tigers, the other club agreed immediately.

The list of games was posted on a big tree in the park. "This will be easy," Hard Boiled said as he chose an event.

The others also picked events that they thought would be easy for them to win. Egg Salad, the last to choose an event, was left with the relay race. She put her name on the bottom of the list as the last runner.

Each day Egg Salad got up early. She dressed and began training for her race.

"One, two, three, four," she counted as she skipped rope.

"What are you doing?" Sunny Side Up asked his sister.

"Getting ready for my race," Egg Salad said.

"Don't bother," Sunny said. "We're going to beat the Tigers easily, so the relay race won't make a difference anyway."

Egg Salad didn't slow down. "You shouldn't be so overconfident," she said. "I'm going to work out every day so I can be the best I can possibly be."

The day of the contest arrived at last. The first event was the pie eating contest.

"Go!" Egg Cream shouted.

Hard Boiled and Butchy of the Tigers each devoured their first pie.

After the second pie, Hard Boiled suddenly got up from the table holding his stomach.

"The winner is Butchy," shouted the Tigers.

Egg Cream and Egg Nog were in the ring toss, the next event. "We always do well at the ring toss," Egg Cream said to Egg Nog who nodded in agreement.

But Egg Cream's first toss missed, and so did Egg Nog's. When the game was over, the Tigers had won again and the score was 2-0!

The next event was the sack race. Halfway around the track, the Tigers were ahead. "Don't worry," Sunny Side Up said. "We'll win this one."

"Maybe we should have trained like Egg Salad did," Over Easy said as they struggled to the finish line to beat the Tigers at last.

Only the relay race was left.

"Ready, set, go!" and the race began.

Over Easy ran around the track and stayed even with the Tiger runner. Then Hard Boiled ran. He got just a little bit ahead of the Tiger's second runner. By the third runner, the Scrambled Eggs looked as if they could tie the contest.

Then it was Egg Salad's turn.

Egg Salad ran as fast as she could and reached the finish line before the Tiger runner was halfway around the track! The Challenge Day was a tie!

The Scrambled Eggs hoisted Egg Salad onto their shoulders. "We're lucky one of us was smart enough to get ready for the games," Hard Boiled said. "We've learned a lesson from you, Egg Salad."

"We've all learned a lesson," she said proudly. "And that is that we Scrambled Eggs always do our best when we work together."